The Pantomime Cat

~ & ~

Mrs Dilly's Duck

Published in 2003 by Mercury Books London
An imprint of the Caxton Publishing Group
20 Bloomsbury Street, London WC1B 3JH

Designed and produced for Mercury Books
by Open Door Limited, Langham, Rutland

Printed in China

Title: The Pantomime Cat & Mrs Dilly's Duck
ISBN: 1 904668 22 4

The Pantomime Cat

~ & ~

Mrs Dilly's Duck

MERCURY BOOKS
LONDON

The Pantomime Cat

M ollie! John!" called Mummy. "Where are you? I want you for a minute."

The two children were playing out in the garden. They ran in. "I hear that old Mrs. Jones isn't well," said Mummy. "She can't go out and do her shopping. Now I think it would be very nice if you two children did her errands for her each day until she is better."

"Oh, Mummy, I don't like Mrs. Jones!" said Mollie. "She always looks so cross!"

"And she never gives anyone a penny, or a biscuit, or a sweet, or anything," said John.

"You don't do kind things for the sake of pennies or sweets," said Mummy. "You know that. You do it because it is good to be kind. You like me to be kind to you?"

"Yes," said Mollie. "We love you for it, Mummy! All right. We'll go – won't we, John!"

They were good- hearted children, so each day at ten o'clock in the morning they ran up the hill to Mrs. Jones's little cottage, knocked on the door and asked her what errands she wanted running.

Mrs. Jones never seemed very pleased to see them, and certainly she never gave them anything, not even a sweet out of her peppermint tin. She was not a very kind old lady and, although the children were polite to her, and always ran her errands cheerfully, they thought she was a cross old thing, and were glad when they had finished going to the grocer's, the baker's and the fishmonger's each day.

It was the Christmas holidays, and circuses and pantomimes were in every big town. There was a pantomime in the town where Mollie and John lived too, and children often stopped outside the big theatre and looked at the pictures.

It's Dick Whittington and his Cat," said Mollie. "Last year it was Aladdin and the Lamp. I do wish Mummy would take us John."

But Mummy had said no, she hadn't enough money for all of them. Perhaps they would go next year.

"You said that last year Mummy," sighed Mollie.
"I do wish we were rich! I'd love to go every night
and see Dick Whittington and his
clever cat. A girl I know has been,
and she says the cat is ever so big
and so funny that she laughed till
she couldn't laugh any more!"

"Now it's ten o'clock," said Mummy.
"Off you go to Mrs. Jones. You won't have to do her
errands much longer because
she can walk quite well now. You have been
good children to run them so cheerfully."

Off went Mollie and John up the hill. They knocked at Mrs. Jones's door and went in. She was sitting at the table, sewing something with a big needle.The children looked at it.
It was a strange thing she was
sewing – like a big, black fur
rug – with a cat's head. "Whatever is that?"
asked Mollie, in surprise.

"Always asking questions!" grumbled the disagreeable old woman. "It's the cat skin my son wears in the pantomime. Didn't you know he was the Cat in Dick Whittington this year?"

"Oh, no!" cried both children in delight. "How perfectly lovely!"

"Hmmm!" said Mrs. Jones, snapping off her thread. "Not so very lovely, I should think – nasty hot thing to wear every night for hours on end. Hmmm! Now listen – my son wants this cat costume this morning before eleven, so pop down now straightaway and say you've brought his costume. That's all I want you to do to-day. After this morning I can do my own shopping, so I won't be seeing you any more."

She wrapped
up the parcel and
the children sped off.
"Mean old thing!" said
Mollie. "Never even said
thank you to us! I say!
What fun to be going in at
the stage door of the theatre!
We might see some fairies –
you know – the ones that sing and dance
in the pantomime!"

They soon arrived at the stage door
and asked the old man there for Mr. Jones.
"Go up the stairs and knock on the second door on
the right," said the old chap. Mollie and John ran
up the stone steps and knocked on the second door.
"Come in!" shouted someone – and in they went.

A round, jolly-faced man was sitting in front of
the mirror. He smiled when he saw them.
"Hallo!" he said. "Have you brought my
cat skin? Thanks awfully! I say are you
the two children who have been running
errands for my mother all this time?"

"Yes," said Mollie shyly.

"And I guess she never said thank you did she? Or gave you a penny between you," 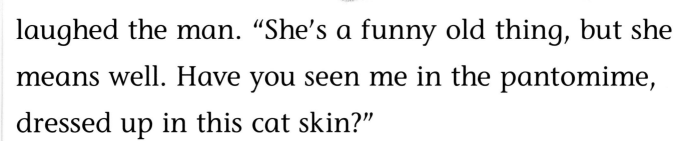 laughed the man. "She's a funny old thing, but she means well. Have you seen me in the pantomime, dressed up in this cat skin?"

"No, we haven't," said John. "Mummy can't afford to take us this year – but, oh, you must look lovely! I wish we could see you!"

"Well, you shall!" said the jolly man, unwrapping the parcel. "You shall have free tickets every night of the week, bless your kind little hearts! That's your reward for being kind to someone who never said a word of thanks! I've some free tickets to give away – and my mother never wants to use them – so you shall have them! Would you like that?"

"Oh, yes!" shouted the children, their faces red with delight. "Yes, yes, yes! We shall see Dick Whittington – and the fairies – and you – and everything else! Oh, what luck!"

Well, it all came true – they did see the pantomime, every night of the week! The jolly man gave them their tickets and, oh, how they loved every minute of it!

"The cat is the best and funniest of all!" said Mollie and John. "We do love him! And we are proud of knowing him, Mummy! Fancy knowing the pantomime cat! All the other boys and girls wish they were us!"

"Ah! You didn't know you were running errands for the pantomime cat's mother, did you?" said Mummy. "You never know what will happen when you do a kindness!"

Mrs. Dilly's Duck

Mrs. Dilly had a pet duck. It was large and white and fat, and its name was Jemima. It had a pond all to itself in the garden, and it was very fond of Mrs. Dilly.

One day, when Mrs. Dilly had two friends to tea – Peter Penny and Sally Simple – she told them about her pet duck.

"She's a wonderful creature," she said proudly.

"She comes when she's called, and she can shake or nod her head when you ask her questions!"

"Good gracious!" said Peter Penny.

"Call her now," said Sally Simple.

"Jemima, Jemima, Jemima!" cried Mrs. Dilly. The duck was swimming on the pond, but she heard Mrs. Dilly's voice. She swam to the edge, climbed out, waddled down the path and in at the door.

"Quack-quack!" she said.

"Oh, you clever thing," said Peter Penny.

"Do you love your mistress?" said Sally Simple.

Jemima nodded her feathery head twice.

"Do you like worms?" asked Peter Penny.

Jemima nodded her head hard.

"Quack, quack, quack!" she said excitedly.

"Would you like to come home with me?"
asked Sally Simple.

Jemima shook her head six times. She was much too fond of Mrs. Dilly to want to leave her.

"You're a dear, clever thing!" said Peter Penny, and he held out half of his cake to Jemima. The duck had never tasted cake before and she took it in her beak and gobbled it down eagerly. "Quack" she said, looking up for more. "Quack!"

Sally Simple gave her a bit of bread and butter with raspberry jam on it. Jemima gobbled it up. Ooooh! It was good! Then Mrs. Dilly laughed and held out a ginger biscuit. Jemima gobbled that too. This was better than worms, and better than frogs!

"Now, that's enough," said Mrs. Dilly. "Off you go back to the pond, Jemima." But the duck didn't want to go. It was nice to be made a fuss of, and how she loved the cake and biscuits and bread and butter! She rubbed her soft head against Peter Penny's knee, and he stroked her.

"Do sell her to me any time you are tired of her," said Peter Penny.

"Or to me," said Sally Simple. "I'd love to have a duck like this!"

Mrs. Dilly shooed Jemima out of the warm kitchen and shut the door. "I don't expect I'd ever want to part with her," she said.

Now Jemima the duck had been so excited over her petting and the titbits she had had, that the next day she thought she would go to the kitchen again and see if there were any more treats to be had. So she left the pond and waddled to the kitchen.

The door was open. Jemima went in. Mrs. Dilly had just washed over the floor and it was clean and shining. Jemima's feet were muddy and wet. They left dirty marks all over the floor.

Jemima stood on her toes and looked on the table. There was a cake there, just baked. Jemima took two or three pecks at it. It was very good.

Just then Mrs. Dilly came bustling into the kitchen. When she saw her nice clean floor all marked by Jemima's dirty feet she was very angry. But she was even angrier when she saw her new cake pecked to bits!

"Oh, you naughty duck! Oh, you rascally creature!" she cried, clapping her hands at Jemima and shooing her to the door. "Don't you ever do this again!"

But you know, once Jemima had found what a pleasant place the kitchen was, always with something good in the larder or on the table, she used to waddle there every day.

Mrs. Dilly tried to remember to keep the door shut, but she hadn't a very good memory, and every time she left it open, Jemima was sure to waddle in!

The things that naughty duck ate! A string of sausages, a cherry-pie, a pound of chocolate biscuits, and even a large cucumber! Mrs. Dilly got crosser and crosser.

   "Now, Jemima, the very next time you come in here, dirtying my kitchen and stealing my food, I shall take you to Peter Penny," she said.

But that afternoon what did she do but leave her door open again, and of course in waddled Jemima and gobbled up a jam tart in the larder!

Mrs. Dilly was very cross. She put on her shawl and hat, tied a string round Jemima's leg, and set off to get the train to Peter Penny's. Jemima was miserable, but she had to go.

Mrs. Dilly took a ticket for herself and one for Jemima. Then she bought a paper and sat down on a seat to wait for the train. She tied Jemima's string to the seat.

Soon, with a roar and a clatter, the train came in.

Jemima was frightened and went under the seat. Mrs. Dilly folded her paper, thinking hard about what she had been reading, and ran to the train. She forgot all about Jemima!

She got into the carriage and the train went off. Mrs. Dilly read her paper again. She got out at the next station and set off for Peter Penny's house. Peter was in the garden, working.

"Good-day," he said to Mrs. Dilly.

"What have you come along here for?"

"I've brought my duck for you," said Mrs. Dilly. "She's such a nuisance, dirtying my kitchen and stealing food.

"Oh, good!" said Peter Penny, "Where is she?"

Mrs. Dilly looked round
for Jemima – but,
of course, she wasn't
there! She was still
in the station!

"Bless us all!" cried
Mrs. Dilly. "I've
left her by the
station seat. How forgetful I am!
I must go back and bring her another day."

Well, when she had journeyed back by train to her own station, there was no duck there! Jemima had got tired of hearing trains thundering in and out of the station and had pecked her string in half. Then she had waddled solemnly home, quacking to herself all the way.

When she got back to her garden she had seen that the kitchen door was open as usual. So when Mrs. Dilly arrived back in a flurry, wondering wherever her poor duck had gone to, she found Jemima standing on the kitchen rug, her head tucked into her wing, fast asleep – and the lettuces, tomatoes, and radishes were all missing out of the larder!

"This is too bad, Jemima, too bad!" cried Mrs. Dilly, almost in tears. She took a broom and swept the surprised duck out of the kitchen. "I'll take you to Peter Penny to-morrow as sure as my name is Dilly."

So the next morning Mrs. Dilly tied the string round Jemima's leg one more and hurried to the station. She did not even sit down on the seat this time, in case she forgot Jemima again.

She jumped into the train and Jemima had to go too. The frightened duck crept under the seat and lay there whilst the train rumbled on. She was too afraid even to quack.

Mrs. Dilly nodded her head and slept. When the train drew up at the station the porter put his head in at the window and bawled loudly: "Change here! Change here!"

Mrs. Dilly woke with a jump. She bundled herself out and, rubbing her sleepy eyes, went to the station door to give up her ticket. Then off she went to Peter Penny's.

But she had forgotten Jemima again. The duck
was still hiding under the carriage seat. She did not
dare to come out.

She stayed there
till the engine was
shunted to the back
of the train, ready
to go off home once
more, for this station
was the last one on the
line. The train clattered off.

When it stopped at Jemima's own station the duck
waddled out from under the seat.

Someone opened the door. Jemima jumped out as the passenger was getting in – what a shock he got to see a large duck struggling by him! Jemima gave an anxious quack and waddled out of the station gate. She set off for home.

As for Mrs. Dilly, she soon arrived at Peter Penny's again. "I've brought Jemima as I promised," she said.

"Good!" said Peter Penny. "Bring her in." But there was no duck there to bring in!

"Lawkamussy, I've left her in the train this time!" said Mrs. Dilly, and she hurried back to the station. But the train had gone, so she had to catch the next, worrying all the time about where Jemima had gone.

But she needn't have worried, for Jemima was safely in the kitchen, gobbling up all the flowers out of the vases. Really, you never knew what the duck was going to eat next!

When Mrs. Dilly got home she was very angry indeed. "I'll take you to Sally Simple's this very afternoon!" she scolded. "I don't like to go to Peter's again, for he will laugh at me – but I'll take

you to Sally's and leave you there, as sure as there is butter on bread."

So that afternoon once more Jemima had a string tied to her leg and once more she set off down the road, this time to Sally Simple's. They didn't go by train, because Sally's was not very far away. They went through the park, where the children were playing, Jemima following solemnly, waddling on her flat feet.

Mrs. Dilly's shoe-lace came undone. She stopped near some railings, and tied Jemima's string there. There were other strings tied there too – the strings of kites flying high in the air.

It was a windy day and the children in the park had brought out their kites.

Once they had them high in the air they had tied the strings safely to the railing, so that the kites might fly high, whilst they went off to play ball.

Mrs. Dilly tied up her shoe. Then she untied a string from the railing and set off. But dear old Mrs. Dilly didn't look to see that her string was the right one – and she had untied a kite-string! So off she went, very solemnly, with a kite flying high in the air behind her! How everyone stared!

Sally Simple lived just near the park. Mrs. Dilly went down a street, still flying the kite without knowing it, and knocked at Sally's door.

"Who's there?" cried Sally. "I'm just doing my hair."

"It's Mrs. Dilly," said Mrs. Dilly. "I've brought my bad duck to you. I don't want her anymore."

"Bring her in, then – bring her in," said Sally, and she opened the door, with her hair down her back. How she stared when she saw the kite flying behind Mrs. Dilly.

"Why are you flying a kite?" she asked.

"I'm not flying a kite!" said Mrs. Dilly, amazed. She looked round for Jemima – and to her enormous astonishment saw that the string went up into the air!

"It must be that Jemima has flown up high in the sky," she said, pulling at the kite. "It can't be a kite, Sally. It must be Jemima flying up there – and yet she didn't have such a long string."

Sally pulled at the string and the kite came down. "It's a kite, Mrs Dilly," said Sally. "Well, it's a funny thing that a duck can turn into a kite, but there it is – it seems to have happened!"

Mrs. Dilly's Duck

Mrs. Dilly was so puzzled that she didn't even remember to say good-bye. She turned and went home, leaving the kite behind her, where it was found by its owner a little while afterwards. Of course Mrs. Dilly didn't find Jemima in the park, for someone had untied the duck and she had waddled home thankfully. When Mrs. Dilly got home she saw Jemima eating the apples out of the fruit dish.

"It seems that I'm not to get rid of you after all, Jemima," said Mrs. Dilly sadly. "I must put up with you. If only I could remember to shut my back door everything would be quite all right! Oh – I know what I'll do! I'll get a cat – and then you will be too frightened to come into the kitchen any more!"

So she got a big white cat called Snowy, and it sat in front of the kitchen fire and warmed its toes. At first Jemima was much too scared to come indoors – but do you know what she is doing now? She is making friends with Snowy the cat, and in no time at all she'll be into the kitchen again, gobbling up all the food in the larder – and I shouldn't be surprised if Snowy doesn't help her! Poor Mrs. Dilly! I wonder what she'll do then, don't you?

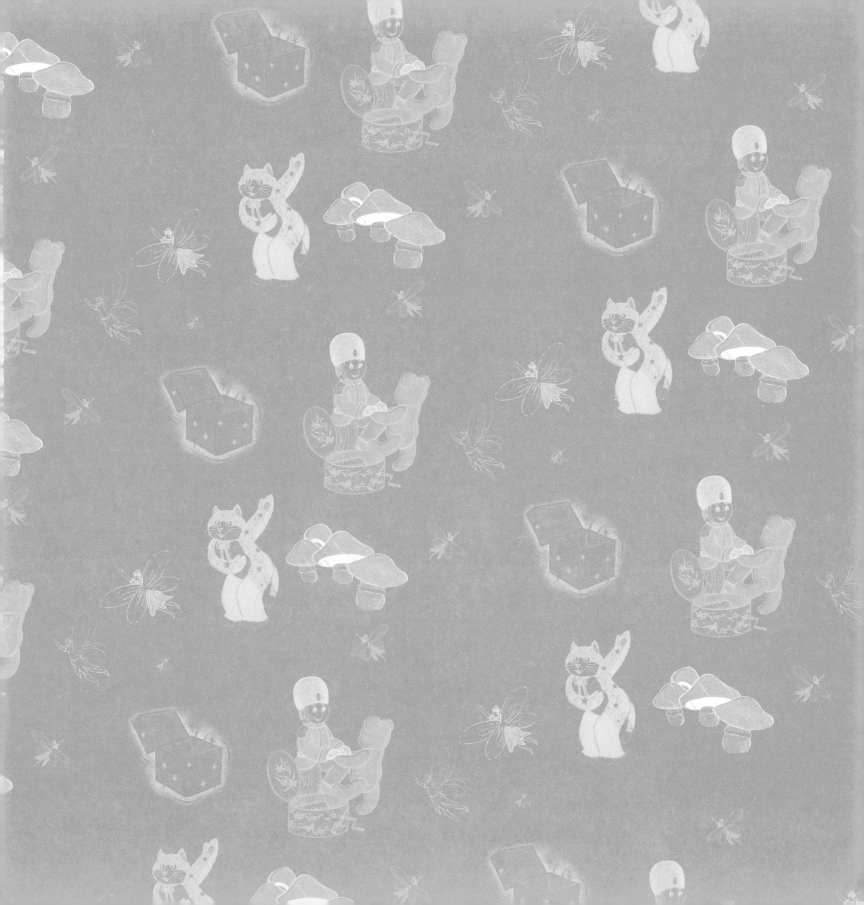